THE HISTORY USHERETTE'S
SECOND SEAT, THIRD ROW

BY

SARAH MILLER WALTERS

Prologue

It is late August in 1944. In London and the south east of England, the doodlebug summer is approaching its end. Mornings are becoming crisper. From over the North Sea a new, faster and more deadly rocket will soon be launching in the direction of the city. Its inhabitants – and its visitors – continue on with their business – aware only of the imminent change of season. Every hour the Thames bridges are thronged with people – none of whom can ever be quite sure that they will survive to make the return crossing. But still they all swarm across Waterloo Bridge, optimistic and determined to complete their errands and carry out their work.

Each week, reels of film in metal canisters make this journey towards the Regal Cinema. The delivery boy's errand is as important as anyone else's. He delivers morale and ninety minutes of escapism to the bombed and bereaved. This week, the metal canisters contain a film called "A Canterbury Tale". The film and advertising posters are delivered into the hands of Mr William

Turner – Manager of the Regal since it was opened in 1935. He gives the posters a glance. Dennis Price, Eric Portman – not a bad offering this week. William Turner feels some respect for these actors – Eric Portman in particular seems to be a no-nonsense northern chap and a fine actor. He resolves to make an effort to see as much of this film as he can. The reels are delivered to the projection room, while William arranges the newspaper adverts.

Regal Cinema.

Continuous Programme from 1.00pm.

A Canterbury Tale.

But people will come, whether he advertises or not. William Turner knows that it is his cinema that is the main attraction. It is a place to escape to, to shut out the harsh daylight, a place where you can put off going back to your wrecked or disjointed home. He isn't always so astute. Let us see if he is correct this time.

The Teacher's Tale

Miriam settled into the cinema seat stiffly, the rough velveteen poking through the thin cotton of her trousers. Her legs were restless but her body had decided to force her to stop walking. The cinema became her stopping place on a whim. It was the title of the film now showing that had drawn her in, away from her dusty plodding reverie. A Canterbury Tale. A film evoking Chaucer and set in England's garden. An attractive young woman on the poster too. What she didn't want to see were Americans, America. Miriam was entirely sick of the lot of them. A film that didn't mention the war at all would have been even better, although the girl on the poster looked like she was Land Army. But an escape from London might still be enough to temporarily soothe.

By the start of the main feature, her nerves began to settle down. Then, after the pastoral introduction, the voice on the train. It tightened her half unravelled nerves again. A bloody Yank turning up in the middle of an English film! Would you credit it? You couldn't get away from them. They were like some kind of lice plaguing the body of England. She had half a mind to get up and walk out of the film. But she was settling down to it now. Perhaps he would only appear in this one scene. But those few words had served to bring it all up again for Miriam's mind to churn over. Anne's story. And then Rose. Proof of them all coming over here and wading right in where they were not wanted. The pain that they had caused. They were devils, every last one.

Anne's letter to Miriam had arrived from Preston just the day before. Her words were as usual brief and gave little in the way of factual information, but Miriam sensed upset. They had been through teacher training together then worked in the same school for some time, sisters of the chalkface. It was marriage that had finally moved Anne away to Lancashire, and made her leave teaching behind. Though much good that had done her. Her husband was now in the Middle East somewhere, the precise location unknown. Anne's letter announced an imminent return to London for a visit to her parents. Could Miriam meet her at Euston sometime today to share a hot tea after the expected torture of the journey?

Even if there had been things to do, Miriam would have moved them to make time for Anne. But she was only wasting the days until school began again. The fact that one of those doodlebugs could land on one's head at any moment gave heightened importance to seeking out friends and pleasure. She had already decided to spend much of the week doing as much sitting about drinking tea as her rations would allow. September and school would bring unbearable strains; children with dead parents to jolly along; children who didn't return at all and their bereft playmates. Even the school itself might have gone by next week. A few hours at Euston station waiting for Anne's train (for heaven knew when it might arrive) was a perfect plan. She observed greetings and farewells, scrabbles for tickets and attempts to get through the barrier without one. Newspapers were consumed without guilt until the Carlisle train edged in, bellowing out a sigh of relief at the buffer stop.

The women chose to leave the Euston Road behind and head for Soho, the place of their receding youth. As respectable schoolteachers the frisson of the back alleys around town always lured them in, delivering momentary rebellious delight. They agreed on a dingy little restaurant, where the walls were yellow and the carpet sticky. Sliding into a torn banquette, they used Anne's suitcase as a footrest and wondered what there might be to eat. Anne looked exhausted, ill even. Miriam had told her so.

"What's keeping you awake then dear? Surely those damn doodlebugs don't get as far as Preston?" she settled back, ready to hear a tale of a lost husband. Surely her troubles must be connected to him. Either that or the in-laws were plaguing her, making unreasonable demands. Miriam was glad that she would never have either. But Anne began to speak of an American airbase near to where her parents in law lived. Miriam immediately, silently, assumed that Anne had been horribly lax in her moral conduct. A Yankee airman, of course it would be. What the hell was the attraction of these people? They looked just like our own men; all they had was a fancy accent and chewing gum. Oh Anne! How bloody brainless. Anne continued with her story, oblivious to the judgement. Last week, one day when the weather was bad, a couple of planes had taken off from this airbase. One tried to turn back. It ended up crashing into the village school. A whole summer school class and its teachers burned to ash. Small children too, the very littlest. She took a breath, a long drink from the chipped cup that had been presented to her by a tiny waitress. Both women stared silently at the tea ringed table top.

"This is why I'm home for a while. I needed to see my own Mother again. And you of course." She squeezed her friend's hand and noticed the line of a tear through her face powder. "Oh Mim, we mustn't let it make us weep today. I hear that rockets are falling out of the sky at all times of the day down here. They must be landing in all sorts of places…schools, hospitals? One can't get emotional about them all."

Miriam nodded. "From what one picks up on the street or the bus. The reports in the newspapers are next to useless. They think it keeps up morale to keep us ignorant. I'm not so sure about that theory."

"And what about your own personal morale, Mim darling?"

"Not good, dear. Not good at all. All these bloody Yanks are getting on my nerves. Do you know, I thought that you were about to spin me a yarn about falling in love with one of them just now. Half the women are obsessed with them and what you've told me just makes it all so much worse. What a bunch of damn idiots! Barging about, sticking their oar into our business. Killing our children for God's sake!"

"Oh Mim. Where is all this anger coming from? It's something to do with Rose isn't it?"

Miriam nodded and lit a cigarette. "She left me. Decided to be a GI bride."

"She went and got married? Oh Lord, how awful!"

"Couldn't even tell me face to face, she left me a note thanking me for everything, and saying that it was time to grow up and be her age."

"Time to grow up! I thought that you and she were going to be together for good…weren't you thinking of opening a private school between you after the war finished?"

"Yes. I was…still am serious about it. It would have been the perfect thing for us to be able to live our days together. But it seems that she was just humouring me. I don't know how to move on from that Anne. What can I do?"

Miriam began to search her satchel for a handkerchief. It was unfortunate that at that particular moment, two American soldiers walked into the restaurant and found the two women in their line of vision. Their banquette was half empty and the two young ladies looked to be in need of some cheery company. Of course two lonely guys in London were going to approach them.

"Excuse me ladies?"

It was a simple phrase but it appeared to launch Miriam up as high as a Flying Fortress. Anne didn't quite catch what her friend said to the two men. It came out as a growl more than a language of any kind. Something akin to her Father-in-law's Jack Russell when it had sight of that rat behind the coal shed. Without another word, the two men touched their caps and went to sit against the opposite wall.

Miriam and Anne sat in silence until their food arrived – a salad served with the tiniest lump of soap-like cheese. Their conversation resumed as they began to pick at what might have been shredded cabbage.

"So, they might be allowing married women to teach again it seems. You could come and run that school with me instead."

"Are you serious about that?"

"Yes, why not?"

"Just checking. Preston certainly holds no delights for me, I would be glad to leave the place."

"Ah, but you'll be turning into a housewife again when the war ends."

"Perhaps I will. Perhaps I won't. It's been so long since I heard anything…I'm beginning to think that he's lost."

"Really? I'm sorry for you."

Anne drew herself up "Well, as my Mother in law would say 'chin up, lass!' "

She began to recount some more of her newly acquired Lancastrian wisdom until their plates and cups stood empty. Miriam approached the cash desk while Anne gathered her belongings. As she moved towards the door she gave what she hoped was an apologetic look in the direction of the Americans. However, they were paying rapt attention to the waitress, who grinned bashfully as she hugged an empty tray to her bosom.

Anne and Miriam stepped out into the open air, where they found little relief from the stuffiness that they had just endured in the restaurant.

"I can smell the Thames!" Anne told Miriam, delighted at the familiar old miasma. "I must go and visit the old ditch before I go to Mother's. Shall we have a walk down to the Embankment?"

"Alright. We'll go to Charing Cross then I'll put you on a bus."

They headed for Charing Cross Road, receiving a faceful of fumes and hot air as they turned the corner. Miriam went over what Rose had done and said again while Anne listened, patiently aware that there was no one else that Miriam could tell.

"When did all this happen?"

"Two months ago exactly. I don't know how long she'd been seeing this Yank of hers, but she'd been doing it in secret. That just proves that she knew it was wrong, that she was hurting me. Her letter made it sound like we'd just been sharing rooms instead of our lives and our plans."

"Poor Mim, you've been bottling it all up too. All this time. You must be tired."

"I think we all are. Everything's in confusion."

They reached Charing Cross station and strolled westwards, trains clanking across the Thames behind them. Even the metalwork of the bridge sounded like it had just about given up. Anne turned back to watch the bustle, her eyes flicking back towards the Thames as it flowed towards the sea. She took hold of Miriam's sleeve and directed her to look up. Her first sighting of a doodlebug. The missile made its way over the City, the droning of the engine stuttering into a dying cough. They watched, silently gripping the parapet, as the rocket dived nose first into the shops and offices, sending up a great cloud of dust.

"I wouldn't be surprised if that was Euston." Anne shook her head.

"Camden, definitely." Miriam agreed.

They continued their walk, moving away from the scene, feeling the dust raining onto their hats and shoulders. All conversation stopped. Miriam put Anne on a bus, which limped its way westwards, full of numb faces and half empty shopping baskets. They promised to meet again the next day, if they were still here. Miriam began to walk over Waterloo Bridge, heading south, even further into Doodlebug territory. She walked until she could go no further, settling at last into the cinema seat.

It was no bit part for the bloody Yank, he didn't go away. His droning voice continued to grate on her nerves, so much so that she could hardly get past it to follow the plot. Perhaps it was time to give up – on today at least. Time to find a train station and get back home to the suburbs. To sit alone and make her plans in the dark.

The GI's Tale

The waitress in the restaurant was bright and friendly, which certainly made up for the cold shoulder that they received when they first walked in. Sometimes it was difficult to know where you were with these people. Some of them went out of their way to welcome you and to soothe your homesick feelings. Others looked right through you – or even worse, told you outright that they didn't like you.

John and Bob tried their best to understand the two ladies that had turned down their offer of company. With these bombs falling all over the place you didn't know what they were going through. Maybe the one who snapped at them had just lost her husband. But you had to try. London could be such a lonely place when you didn't know it too well. But it seemed like that sweet little waitress was going out of her way to make it up to them. She stayed by their table chatting for so long that Bob began to wonder if she might get into trouble with her boss. She looked so young, like it might be a big deal if the manager shouted. John however had rather a different thought in his head concerning the waitress. He made it his own concern to find out what time she finished, which turned out to be in thirty minutes time. They made their arrangements while Bob was left stirring his drink. Finally the girl was called away; John leaned back in his chair and grinned over at Bob.

"You don't mind, do you? That was too good a chance to pass on."

"I guess not. But you could have asked her if she had a friend or something…"

"You're a married man, Robert Macdonald, and don't you forget that. I'm supposed to be helping you to stay faithful, remember!"

"Yeah yeah. Well, what am I supposed to do while you go and do your thing?"

"Go to the movies or something. Want me to give you a shilling for some popcorn?"

"Oh sure popcorn's going to be on the menu."

The two men arranged to meet at Victoria railway station when it became time for them to make their way back to the base. John took the young waitress' arm and they set out northwards with just a brief farewell for Bob. She was going home to get changed, and then she would show John all the delights that Camden had to offer. Bob decided to take a good look around, see what turned up. He wasn't too worried about finding his way back to the station, he was certain that someone would direct him, so he set out eastwards. He found himself on Charing Cross Road, where he sauntered into a bookshop and picked up a slim collection of love poetry. This would be the very thing to present his wife with when he returned home. A poetry book all the way from London. How could any wife not be impressed? Bob said so to the old man who took his payment. He was about to respond with some piece of information about his own wife when he stopped abruptly and gestured to Bob to be silent too. The drone and splutter of the doodlebug got louder; there was soon no mistaking it.

"Come and get under the counter!" the old man yelled out as he ducked himself underneath the cash register. Bob joined him among the cobwebs and piles of unsaleable books. He knocked a mouldy pile of

Shakespeares to the floor as the impact was felt, perhaps a mile or so away.

"That was a near one." The old man eased his joints into a standing position and began to assess the ceiling and the shelves for any damage. Bob restacked the Shakespeares and brushed a cobweb off his uniform.

"Thanks for the shelter. That kind of thing must be setting your nerves on edge. Don't you get any kind of warning siren?"

"Usually yes, but sometimes one gets through before they can do anything about it. We're all starting to listen out for them all the time now, without even thinking about it. Anyway, no sign of any damage this time. We live to read another day."

"Well, good luck." Bob touched his cap and left the bookshop. A thought occurred to him that people may be in need of help where the rocket had landed. Perhaps he ought to go and see what he could do. He followed the sound of the ringing bells and walked towards the column of smoke the continued to rise up, funnelling debris down onto the top of his cap. London seemed determined to send him back to the base covered in filth.

He walked the subdued streets, past the British Museum and through squares, all empty of their railings and grass. A young boy covered in a coating of dust sprinted past him, his eyes wide and staring straight ahead. Bob turned a corner and found the road where the rocket had landed. It was a shopping street, and whatever stores had stood halfway down were now annihilated. Guarding the mass of uniforms, vehicles and shattered glass was a police officer with a weary expression and a large Edwardian style moustache. Surely this guy should be retired by now, Bob thought.

"You can't come down here sir. Can't you see what's happened?"

"Well, I just wondered if I could be of any help to you?"

"No, no. Our lads know what they're doing. They don't need anyone else getting in their way thank you all the same. Move along now please."

The policeman turned to speak to a pair of anxious old ladies who stood at the corner with their empty shopping baskets. Bob turned around, feeling like he was turning his back on the dead and injured. The WVS were in the process of setting up a tea van as he stopped to brush his cap off. A thin old woman beckoned him over to her.

"Come on soldier, the urn's just about ready. Let's get you a nice strong cup of tea."

Bob resisted an eye-roll. Tea, the British antidote to everything. He could not understand the attraction. But what Bob was beginning to understand was that it was rude to refuse. Bomb these people out of their homes and they carried on singing. Turn down the offer of a cup of tea and watch them silently mark you down as some kind of monster. Bob edged over to the woman, unsure what to do. The tea van wasn't there for him. What was the British view on obtaining tea under false pretences? He decided to explain that, kind though the offer was, he was only a passer-by.

"No matter, dear. You still look like you could do with one. It shakes you up all this business, even if you don't realise it at the time." She handed Bob a steaming mug and began to chat to him about his home. He leaned up to the van's pull out counter, unaware that a few yards behind him covered bodies were beginning to be stretchered from the rubble. The first body to be brought out and placed in a van was that of his buddy, John. Next came that of the waitress, whose body had lain directly underneath.

As people who really needed tea and sympathy came up to the WVS van, Bob slipped away. He turned around and headed back for Charing Cross Road, finding Trafalgar Square instead. Soon, he found himself by the Thames and he hung around the Embankment for a while, watching the scene. It soon occurred to him that it would be the most exciting thing to tell his wife that he had actually walked across the river. He took Hungerford Bridge and walked alongside the trains, turning again when he reached the south shore to marvel at his path. It was a shame that there was no-one with him to share the view. Waterloo station beckoned him in with its bustle, but he continued on into south London in search of a movie. John was right, he had concluded, he would be happier lost in a picture for a while. He reckoned on another two hours before he should begin his search for Victoria Station. Plenty of time. Bob wondered what John was doing right now. He might be laid out somewhere with that waitress. If that was the case, then he would be in a stupid mood all the way back to the base. If not then he'd be in a terrible mood. Either way, he was going to be hard work later on. Might as well kick back and get some rest.

There was nothing like a relaxing smile from the box office, in fact Bob wondered if he should apologise for waking the old lady up. But the usherette made up for the first impression. She smiled as he walked into the auditorium, skilfully casting herself in the torchglow. There was certainly something to see there, a curvy body and a pretty face framed by blonde curls. The face though belonged to a baby. They grew up too quickly around here, Bob concluded. Touching his elbow lightly, she showed him a seat that had been recently vacated. He could still feel the warmth. He settled right back, removing his cap and placing it in his lap. The usherette touched his shoulder and whispered

"If you need anything soldier, just let me know" before melting away in to the dark.

He got the feeling that this film was nearing its conclusion. The woman on the screen had just been told that someone was still alive. Well at least he could sit through it now knowing that there was a happy ending. He tried to shut himself off until the newsreel, then the feature would start all over again. But his eye was caught by the scenes of the Canterbury ruins. They were bombing places like that as much as they were bombing London? It seemed likely that if this war didn't finish soon, then there would be nothing of the old country left. He should see as much of it as he could while he was over here. He wanted to see the churches, the burial places of the great. He would tell John this as soon as he saw him.

The Usherette's Tale

Kay Clarke looked at her watch ostentatiously – not that there was anyone around to observe and admire her style. It was a habit that she'd developed since buying the watch with her first pay packet. It was only a cheap one from Billy down the street but it looked just like one she'd seen Vivien Leigh wear once. It added a touch of glamour to her slender wrists, something that she wanted everyone to notice. She also liked people to know that she had a schedule to keep to. Looking this pretty every day took time.

Her brother was late. Kay plonked herself down on a seat on the third row to wait for him. She was sure that she would be alright walking home on her own but her mother insisted on sending her little brother to collect her at closing time.

"Some people are using this war to get away with murder. And I mean murder", was her mother's standard retort to Kay's complaints. "You're safer in twos." Obviously it didn't occur to her that a passing doodlebug could wipe out both her children at once.

So, every night when her shift was over she had to wait for Tommy to turn up. He didn't have a watch, that was evident. If he didn't come soon she would be turfed out of the cinema when the manager locked up, then have to stand and wait outside when she'd already been on her feet all night.

Kay thought back over the evening's shift. It was a queer film this week. She was having trouble following 'A Canterbury Tale.' All this putting glue in girls' hair – what was that about exactly? He was nice though, the American soldier that starred in it. She'd let him take her home if he asked her nicely. What was it that her Mum's friend Dorothy had read in her tea leaves? A man from overseas would change her life soon. She thought back too to the soldier that she had shown to a seat – somewhere around where she was sitting now. He was lovely looking, and so polite. She'd tried her best to grab his attention but in the end he'd just walked out with a silent nod and a smile at the end of the film. She sat and dreamed that he had waited until closing time especially to talk to her. To pick her up, then place her down somewhere warm and sunny. Kay was particularly on the lookout for a soldier that came from California or Florida. She'd heard that those places were warm enough to grow oranges and grapes. She imagined herself plucking fruit in a huge garden while dressed in the latest bathing suit and began to slip into a reverie.

"Kay! Come on, out we go. I'm locking up." The manager's flat old vowels snapped her back into reality.

"I'm coming, Mr Turner." She heaved herself out of the seat and hobbled towards the exit on stiffened legs. The night air was cool, September was drawing near. A nice pair of nylons would be alright for starters, before she got whisked off to Florida. Just to get her through the winter.

"Still no sign of your brother, Kay?" William Turner looked up and down the street. There were a few loitering, but none of them were Tommy. "Would you like me to walk you as far as the junction?"

Kay would rather walk with anyone other than her manager. They all thought he was a bit strange. It was the way he never looked at you when he spoke, and that funny scar down his cheek and neck. The strangest thing was that nobody knew anything about him and this led them all to conclude that he had a terrible secret. There was much speculation in the ladies' room about what this secret might be. Kay didn't want to be the one that found out while walking past a dark bombsite.

"No, Mr Turner. You get on home and put your feet up. I'm sure that Tommy will be here any minute. He's usually late but he always comes for me."

"Well, if you're sure? There's a nice bright harvest moon to watch over you anyway. Goodnight, Kay."

"Yes, Mr Turner. Goodnight."

Kay began to pace, cursing Tommy for denying her a cup of tea and good sit down. She could have been home now. The doodlebug that landed earlier was over the river they said, he couldn't have been caught in that, surely not. She became conscious of someone approaching from her left. She turned quickly, guarded, only to be offered a cigarette by the moonlit outline of a soldier, an American one.

"You been stood up too, honey?" he drew lazily on his own cigarette and offered Kay a light. She accepted it giddily, unused to smoking and wondering whether it was quite ladylike to be stood almost in the street while doing so.

"Well, I'm just waiting for my brother to come and walk me home. I work here you see." She gestured back to the cinema with her cigarette, so he definitely knew where to find her in future.

"What? Don't you know your way home yet? You look pretty grown up to me."

"It's the dark and the bombsites, you see. Mum insists that we're safer in twos."

"Well for one thing you ought to be used to the dark in your job. And for another what about your brother on his way to fetch you…he's not in twos then."

Kay agreed. "You're very clever. It's true. But you can't argue with her."

"Sure. Well it looks like the young lady who agreed to meet me here isn't going to show up. Would you like me to drive you home?"

"You've got a car?"

"Well, it's more of a truck that I've borrowed. But you're welcome to a ride home in it."

"Really? Oh I'd love to. Oh, but Tommy…that's my brother. What if we pass him and don't see him. He'll worry if I'm not here."

"Okay okay, listen. I'll walk you home and come back for the truck after we've found your brother."

Kay hesitated. She reminded herself that the glueman existed only in the film she'd been watching, he wasn't here in south London. But an American serviceman in uniform…he couldn't be a danger, surely? He wouldn't risk the good name of his country. There was that predication in her tea leaves….what if this was the man to change her life? She really shouldn't turn him down.

"I'm sorry my lady, we haven't been formally introduced, have we? My name is Gustav." He offered his arm to her.

She couldn't hold back a guffaw at his attempt at an English accent. She told him her name and took his arm. They began to walk towards the moon.

"Gustav doesn't sound like a very American name, somehow."

"Well, I was born in Sweden. My family settled in the states when I was a baby."

"Did they settle somewhere hot? What's it like where you're from?"

"Well, I'm from Massachusetts, which is hot in the summer but it gets cool in the winter. But I might settle further south when this is all over."

"I dream of living somewhere that the sun shines all the year round."

"Why do you work in a dark cinema if you love the sunshine so much?"

"Needs must, got a mother and brother to support. Anyway it won't be forever, I'm sure of it."

They arrived at Kay's home, having seen nothing of Tommy on the route. They agreed that Gustav should wait outside while she went in to find out if anything was wrong. She shoved open the back door while he leaned on the wall at the end of the yard. The back door always seemed to warp in the summertime and it made a loud grinding which shook the kitchen. She pushed it closed again and fought her way through the blackout curtain.

Tommy was sat in their mother's armchair, a leg hooked over the arm. Disturbed by the sound of the door, he squirmed himself awake and twisted to look at the clock on the mantelpiece.

"Oh no! Kay!" He rubbed his eyes with his shirt sleeve. "I'm really sorry, I must have nodded off."

"Where's Mum? She should have woken you up." Kay sensed that something was amiss, she peered down the hallway. Her mother's hat and coat were missing from the peg.

"She's at Granddad's. He had a turn for the worse this afternoon. They've got the doctor round there."

"I see. Do you….do you think this is it this time?"

Tommy nodded and rubbed his eyes again.

"Well, at least he's going in his own bed and not under a pile of rubble."

"Sorry, Kay. Glad you got home alright anyway. You won't tell Mum that I forgot, will you?"

Kay smiled at her brother, and traded in her silence for Tommy's discretion over the visitor that she was about to bring in from the back yard. Gustav came in and shared a pot of the tea with them, Tommy discreetly popping out back when it was time to say goodnight. Kay agreed to meet Gustav the following morning before her next shift at the cinema began. He would have to take pot luck with what they did, she told him, but he responded that he didn't mind, as long as she would be there.

The Manager's Tale

William Turner took his responsibilities at the cinema seriously. It was the only part of his life that he could have control over. At home he had Mary and Joy dictating everything that he did. The Home Guard captain revelled in delivering orders at him and his comrades as if they were all still in a trench back in 1918. But when he was at his work, he kept order. He surprised the usherettes with regular uniform inspections. He took a close interest in the box office takings and patrolled the auditorium every morning to ensure that a satisfactory level of cleanliness was maintained. His staff all thought that he was a strange man, he realised that. But a man had to find self-respect somewhere in his life. The scars on his face didn't help him become more beloved. His usherettes were all young, they didn't remember what it was like when the streets had been full of men showing raw flesh. His scars remained visible where other men had been able to cover theirs with their clothes or, in many cases, their coffins. Even those that had survived the trenches with him had seemed to give up on life so easily. His comrades had just about all gone. Mrs James in the box office seemed to tolerate him more than the others, which was odd because she was a woman with little time for other people. But women of her age – well, they knew how it had been.

William's sense of duty was one of the reasons why he came into work so much earlier than everyone else. He could then check that all was in order without hindrance or disturbance. Once he had satisfied himself that his customers would find nothing to complain about, he sat himself down in one of the seats. He would choose a different seat every day, in this way he sought out those seats in need of repair, or perhaps a little lubricant to prevent squeaks. He allowed himself ten minutes of reflection with a cup of tea and a cigarette. On this particular day, he selected the third row for seating inspection. He made himself comfortable. The day was warm, the kind of weather that made you want to seek out some open countryside, climb a hill and find a breeze. This film that they had just started showing, this Canterbury Tale thing, it didn't help; all those scenes out in the fields, kiddies playing by the river. It took William right back to his youth by the Trent, the days spent wading among the weeds and the mossy stones at the river edge. He'd grown up too soon; starting work in the local music hall and watching his elder brother go off to fight a war. By Christmas of 1917 it was his turn to be taken out into France to be shelled and gassed; the next in line for a new family tradition. But he wasn't going to go until he'd married his sweetheart; indeed she had told him that this was going to be necessary. William and his Mary hurried to the pointy red brick chapel one grey morning and left as Mr and Mrs Turner. Mary had been secretly glad of the hurry because she had been working at the munitions factory for long enough. The older girls were losing their looks and she was keen to get out before hers went too.

Baby Joy arrived a few months later and was so named in surprise at William's still being alive and able to attend her Christening. William and Mary gained each other and their baby in the final months of war. But they both lost something too. William lost his looks from a piece of shell in the right hand side of his face. Mary, meanwhile, lost a piece of her mind.

Because she couldn't speak of it, he never fully found out everything that she had seen on the day that the munitions factory had exploded. He had gathered this much, that she had been out one July morning, pushing the infant Joy in her perambulator, when the whole place went up. She had run to her mother's house, the top of the perambulator covered in all kinds of strange debris and had sat in the corner of the kitchen, silently screaming. When at last she had recovered enough of her senses to find her way to her own home, she saw something lying in the road. She had never gathered herself in enough to tell anyone what it was but William had heard tell of body parts strewing the streets. Finally, it was the list of friends who may or may not have been part of that debris that had fallen from the sky; a whole group of yellow-tinged girls that had giggled at the back of the church on their wedding day. There wasn't even enough left of them for a grave each. All this combined to tip Mary into a 26 year silence. William found this to be exceptionally hard work; especially exasperating when she went to great lengths to communicate something through elaborate gestures.

"Speak! Just speak, woman!" he used to yell at her. But he gave that tactic up – it was clear that she never would speak. Joy, as she grew, went in for compensation by rarely ever stopping speaking. She interpreted every one of her mother's gestures to anyone else present and gave a commentary on every domestic development. She refused to ever marry or leave home, telling William that he hadn't enough heart to care for Mary himself. He could barely stand being with them.

He had tried to make Mary normal again; the move to London in 1919, away from the scene of the disaster and towards the better chance of a job for him. He attempted to extend their family many times, convinced that Mary would find her voice again in the throes of childbirth. But that second child did not want to be born. He gave that side of things up because of the lack of encouragement from Mary. Now, he lived for his cinema, his daily escape from the madness of his home. Things had got worse since the war started. Any loud noise had always sent Mary into a panic, so of course the Blitz had caused no end of trouble in their house; hiding under the bed and refusing to come out, Joy, rubbing her hands raw with the continual washing of Mary's drawers. She went missing twice. William came to work earlier every day. He was permanently in dread of his sanctuary taking a direct hit. Where would he go then?

The first two usherettes arrived, breaking William's lonely reverie. He went to make his checks in the box office, pretending that he had not been here all morning while the girls giggled in their cloakroom. He wondered who they were laughing at. An insistent knocking at the window made him look up from the ticket reels. A breathless boy, still in short trousers that were straining at the seams, peered in at him.

"The cinema doesn't open for another half an hour, sonny. You'll have to wait."

"Mr Turner! It's me, Tommy, Kay's brother!"

"Oh yes, so you are." William peered over the top of his spectacles at the lad. He knew that he was about to be told that he would be an usherette down today. What would be the excuse this time? "Well, where is she?"

"She's been attacked, Mr Turner."

"Oh no. On her way home last night was it? I knew I should have insisted on walking her home." He took his spectacles off and rubbed his eyes; something else for his conscience to taunt him with in the middle of the night.

"No, Mr Turner. She got home alright last night. This American soldier walked her home. He seemed to be really nice as well so she let him come and call for her this morning. Mum had given her some money to go and queue up at the grocers and he went with her. Then ten minutes later she came home again with a black eye and blood just pouring down her face, Mr Turner. She looked horrible."

"Go on. What happened to her?"

"She said that they cut across the old bomb site from the Blitz and when they were halfway over he thumped her and ran off with the food money and the coupons and her watch."

"I see." William stared at Tommy a moment and considered his culpability. She wouldn't have met the soldier if he had walked with her. But then again Tommy didn't come to collect her on time. It could be his fault.

"Erm, so Kay can't come to work. Her face is a mess and she won't stop crying either."

"No. I see. Well tell her to take two days off. I'll pop round and see her tomorrow morning, see how she's getting on, shall I?"

"If you want to, Mr Turner. I'll tell her to expect you."

"Good. Now. Do you know where Betty Jones lives?"

"Course I do, Mr Turner."

"Now. Go and ask her to come to work instead of Kay, would you?" He fished for a ha'penny in his pocket and pushed it through the ticket window. "Oh, and Tommy? Tell Kay that I hope she's alright soon."

The Porter's Tale

Betty Jones didn't mind doing an extra shift at the cinema. The family needed the money and, like every other Londoner, she had learned how to carry on with the minimum of sleep. When she heard about Kay's attack, she called out to her sister to come and listen to the tale. Dora Jones had been in the same class at school as Kay, they had been best friends, on and off. Dora came in from the scullery, where she was attempting to get her uniform dry ready for her afternoon shift at the station.

"I'll come back to your house with you, Tommy. I'll sit with her until I have to go to work."

Tommy and Dora made to leave as Betty frantically combed out the pincurls in her hair. "You ought to take her a little something to cheer her up. What have we got?"

"We've got that big onion off Uncle Bill's allotment." Dora suggested.

"Alright, take that. We can always get another next week."

Dora went to unhook the onion from a peg in the scullery. "Kay likes them, doesn't she Tommy?"

"Don't we all?" He eyed the crisp skinned vegetable with a mouth watering hope that his sister would be feeling generous. The pair set off towards Tommy and Kay's home, going over again the incident on the bomb site that morning.

On their arrival, Kay was upstairs and refusing to come out of her bedroom. Dora stood at the bottom of the stairs, calling up persuasive words. The bedroom door remained closed, just the shadow of Kay's feet visible in the line of light underneath it.

"She's brought you an onion! Come on, at least come out and say thanks!" Tommy joined in the persuasion.

But Kay was going to let nobody see her in this particular state, especially not somebody that she had been at school with, who might twist her words and exaggerate her injuries for the benefit of Betty and the other usherettes. Eventually she exchanged a few words with Dora from the shadows behind the bannister to compensate for the onion, making sure to thank her for it so that she didn't take it back with her. Dora left, deciding to head straight for the cinema. It would take her mind off other things before starting work. And it was a good excuse to rest her legs, which tired easily these days.

Dora passed on what little she had discovered about Kay to Mrs James as she purchased her ticket, then took a seat in the third row – near the end in case she needed to dash to the toilet. She wished that she hadn't been in time for the newsreel and the scenes from Europe. That reminded her of her predicament and made her start wondering about a certain person. She closed her eyes and ears to it and felt a wave of nausea creep up; the smell of stale cigarette smoke and the odour of hot August bodies. She went into the toilet and locked herself in a cubicle. It was a long shot, but sometimes she did feel queasy when her monthly curse was just starting. She checked her knickers; nothing. She knew that there wouldn't be anything really. There hadn't been anything last month either, in fact there'd been no bleeding since the end of May. The bile rose in her throat and poured out into the toilet. The tea and crust of toast rejected again. She wiped her face and went back out to see the main feature, intending to lose herself in this, wipe her mind blank before making a definite decision today on what to do next. When to tell her mother and sister; what to say; what her plan was. At least she knew the father's name and regiment. That was something. More than a lot of other girls had, from what she'd seen.

Dora settled down in the same seat and began to watch 'A Canterbury Tale.' She immediately admired Alison the Land Girl. She took no nonsense, worked hard and stood up to the men. Dora found herself wishing that she had joined the Land Army. She had thought about it, when she left school. The open fields and dark quiet nights appealed to her, as a holiday somewhere foreign and exotic. She liked helping Uncle Bill on the allotment too. When she told her mother this one Saturday night, after they had shared a glass of something medicinal to help them through a bombing raid, the old woman hooted like an owl.

"You wouldn't last five minutes my girl, you couldn't dig your way out of a molehill!"

Dora was told that there was plenty of war work to be done within walking distance of her home. Why go away and do it? Stay at home where your mother can look after you. So she stayed at home and got a job at Waterloo Station, portering among the smoke and the crowds. One day she was followed by a handsome country boy as she left the station, who asked her with such a warm smile if she knew of anyone around here who could take him out dancing. He was the one who went off to invade France and left her with this little package. If only she'd had the guts to stand up to her mother. She could be out in the fields now, in Kent like Alison, picking apples and making haystacks. She'd never seen a haystack in real life, they looked like fun.

But it was Waterloo for Dora, and never looked like being anywhere else now. Unless her country soldier came back – which he said he would do. Where was it he came from? One of the shires, one of those that are spelt differently to how they sound; Worcestershire or

Gloucestershire she thought. Perhaps he would get out of France alive then take her and their child back to his shire. Maybe his family house was like Mr Colpeper's, all big windows and a garden full of flowers. As the film closed, Dora learned that Alison got her fiancé back. Perhaps he would come back. He could just be wounded or his letters could just be getting lost in the post like the American soldier's.

Although the film was finished, it wasn't time for Dora to go home. Not yet. She would now sit through the supporting feature and concentrate her mind. It was time to do something, before she reached the stage when the buttons popped off her work tunic. Her mother had to be told and Dora anticipated the response with dread. There would be a rattle of profanities delivered in the Welsh language, followed by accusations of loose morals and an official disowning. Probably best then to tell her just before she went off to work. By the end of her shift she would have calmed down enough to let her back into the house. There would then be demands to know about the father, and what Dora planned to do next. If these plans were to pass muster, it must not involve her mother having to do anything, Dora must prove herself to be independent. She had started saving already. She would use the savings to go away to a home somewhere in the country and have the baby there. Then when her money ran out she would come back to London and go back to work. Somebody would take care of her baby, another young mother with a baby of her own perhaps. In the meantime she would keep on writing to her soldier in the hope that he would get at least one of her letters and know to come straight back to her.

Dora's thoughts were broken by a commotion near the front seats. A man had upset her neighbour Mrs Burns for some reason. Betty was seeing to it – it reminded Dora that she ought to go and tell her Mother now, while Betty was out of the way. It would soon be time for her shift to start at the station. She slid out into the sunshine and plodded home along dusty streets, watching the children playing at hide-and-seek on the bombsite as she passed. Her mother was home from the shops and in a good mood, having obtained a couple of sausages at the butchers. Dora put her uniform on, a quick exit all prepared. She stood in the scullery and pulled her tunic together. The buttons around her bust were starting to gape a little. She looked up and saw her mother watching her.

"When are you going to tell me, Dora?"

"Tell you what?" Dora's hands froze.

"Don't tell me you haven't realised, my girl. You haven't washed any curse rags for the last two or three months and look at you. Blooming, I'd call it. Well?"

"I was going to tell you today."

"And yesterday. And last week too, no doubt."

Dora, her bottom lip trembling, began to cry.

"Scared of your old mother, are you? Come and sit down. You've time for a quick cup of tea before your shift. Or are you off tea? I was when I was having you. Tasted funny."

"It does taste strange. But I'll have some all the same."

"Good. Now what's going on? Out with it all."

Dora told her mother about her soldier and her plans, which did, in the end, make her mother cross.

"Pay someone to look after your child? I'm not good enough to take care of my own grandchild then? Not enough practice you think? And that money is better off in our house let me tell you. This baby won't be cheap. And you can forget going away to have it. Have old Nosy Parker Burns next door think you've got something to hide? You'll have it here, where I can keep an eye on you. There, now get to work. And leave me your soldier's name and regiment and I'll make enquiries."

Dora's mother shooed her out of the door, calling after her as she turned the corner to watch herself with those heavy trunks. She turned back into the house, sat down at the kitchen table and began to cry. The image of her daughter stood in the scullery, nervously tugging at her tunic plagued her. Whether her tears were for joy, apprehension or just the thought of all the years that had passed, she herself had no idea.

The Corporal's Tale

Albert Wilton thought about going off to look for his wife when he was on Victoria Station last night. It was so busy though, and he was so tired. Then he got jostled by a group of American soldiers. One of them said that he had lost his buddy; he was pushing his way through the crowds calling out frantically for someone called John. Albert had got shoved right in the ribs. It had made him feel quite ill and knocked any sense of purpose out of him. So he went to the Home Guard drill instead, put up with the same old rubbish. There'd be no invasion now. Waste of time. Everything was.

As he sipped his breakfast cup of tea he took out the plan of London. He spread it out on the table, turned his back and threw her best coronation spoon over his shoulder. Wherever the handle pointed to, that is where he would find her. It hadn't worked so far, granted, but these things needed practice. One day he would go to a place and she would be there. Today the spoon pointed at Battersea

Park, a trip south of the river for a change. He'd enjoy that.

Of course it wasn't much of a park anymore. It was all allotments, rows of green beans and carrots instead of children playing on the grass. A group of women in headscarves raked and hoed around the plants and Albert began to feel guilty about watching them work. They all looked so tired. But his fingers were bent. And if he got down on his hands and knees to do some weeding, there was a chance that he wouldn't be able to get back on his feet. He wasn't going to find her here. He tottered back to the station and caught the next train into Waterloo. Perhaps she might be there. A station was as good a place as any, considering.

He found a cup of tea – rather weak for his taste, then loitered a while beside the newspaper stand. That was where he saw her, at last. "Ethel!" he called out to her, but she couldn't hear him over the din. He began to follow her towards the station steps. Her coat and hat looked shabby, and he didn't remember seeing them before. But still, the face, the hair, the shape of her calves

– it was Ethel. She left the station and walked briskly down bustling streets. It was all he could do to keep up with her. Eventually she turned into a cinema. He arrived at the box office just as her green coat disappeared through the double doors into the darkness beyond. He panted as he asked for the same ticket as the lady that had just gone in, meeting a harsh stare from the woman who filled the window. He counted out heavy change into the coin tray, and was finally able to follow Ethel inside. He squinted about him, she had by now taken her seat and he couldn't see her. The usherette approached him, her torch playing about the floor.

"Plenty of seats along the back two rows here, sir." Betty Jones told him, briefly sweeping the light along the seat backs to demonstrate.

"I'm looking for my wife." He told her as his eyes sought out the familiar grey bun. She came in a minute ago in a green coat and straw hat.

Betty studied Albert's face. "But the last lady to come in was my neighbour, Mrs Burns. She's not your wife."

Albert took no notice of Betty. He'd spotted Ethel down near the front and began to speed down the stairs towards her. "Ethel! It's me, I'm here!"

The woman sat, straw hat on her lap, absorbed in the newsreel. Albert tugged at her sleeve.

"Ethel! Ethel it's me, Albert!"

The woman turned sharply then drew her arm away from Albert's grasp. "Here, get off. I'm not your Ethel!"

Her voice belted through the newsreel music, a harsh south London accent. It was nothing like Ethel's quiet enunciation. Albert at last knew it was not his wife. He began to weep into his hands, his shoulders shaking violently. There were murmurs all around the auditorium, but no-one knew what to do. Betty took control.

"Come on ducks, come out into the foyer and I'll find you a nice cup of tea." She took his elbow and led him back up the steps and out into the afternoon light. She found him a chair and lowered him onto it as he wiped his face with a grimy handkerchief. The projection boy swerved around them, studying the pair with deep interest.

"Ooh Harry, just go and get this gentleman a nice cup of tea, will you? Strong as you can get it; he's just had a funny turn."

Harry skipped off without a word, too intent on listening to what Betty would say next to answer her.

"Now dear, what's the matter? You lost your wife then? Where did you last see her?"

"I saw her off when she got on the train to go and see her sister."

"Alright, she went to her sister's. What makes you say she's lost?"

"Well, when she was supposed to be travelling back, a doodlebug hit the railway bridge and the train crashed. It was in Kent. They came and told me that they'd found Ethel's handbag in a carriage but that there was no trace of her body."

"I see. Look, Harry's brought your tea. Drink up."

The cup and saucer shook so violently in his hands that Betty had to take away the saucer and hold his hand steady as he drank.

"She's not dead." He continued on when the cup was drained. "She's either lost her memory or someone stole her bag and she wasn't on the train at all. So I have to find her, you see."

"You're not from round here, are you? Don't you think you'd be better waiting for her at home? What if she finds her way back and you're not in?"

"She can wait with a neighbour. But I feel sure that she must have lost her memory so I've got to go out and find her."

"London's a big place though isn't it ducks? Is there anyone I can try and get hold of for you? I mean to come and fetch you?"

Albert shook his head. There was no-one else, only him to go and find her in this teeming city.

"Well, why don't you go in and watch the film while you take a few breaths. You've paid to see it now. It's a nice film, it'll cheer you up."

Albert let Betty guide him to a seat, the second one on the third row. He settled into the seat and watched tanks flying about the fields of Kent. He wished that he had a machine just as fast and agile as that one, one that would take him directly to his Ethel.

This time there was a warning. They had a few minutes to take cover from the doodlebug – if they wanted to. The siren called down the road and a message flashed up on the screen. Most of the audience allowed themselves to be led to the shelter by the usherettes. There had been enough near misses with these flying bombs to make them wary. But William Turner stayed with this cinema, and Albert Wilton stayed too. A few others stirred but then remained in their seats, either too tired or too fatalistic to rouse themselves. The doodlebug glided across the sky then began its staccato stutter above Waterloo Station. It managed another half mile or so before the engine cut out and the rocket tipped then hurtled towards the ground. It exploded efficiently on impact, tearing the cinema in half, tossing the seats into the afternoon sky along with the souls of their fatalistic inhabitants.

Epilogue

When Betty Jones came out into the fresh air at the sound of the all-clear and saw the carcass of the cinema, she realised that Albert Wilton had not been in the shelter with them. It was later confirmed that he had been among the casualties that were dug out of the rubble. She became quite convinced that Albert's wife had been dead after all, and that she had sent her earthly twin to lure her husband up to heaven, where they could be reunited for evermore. It confirmed what Betty thought she knew about the afterlife, and cemented her career as an amateur palmist and clairvoyant. But she was quite wrong in this theory. Mrs Wilton wasn't dead at all, and would continue to live for another two or three decades. Neither would she wish to be reunited with Albert, whom she considered to be an increasingly stifling presence in her life. The visit to her sister in Kent had been genuine, but what she had failed to mention to Albert was her frequent liaisons with her sister's local ARP warden while she was down there. The train crashing on her way home presented her with a very tempting if impulsive opportunity which she took – finally realising that happiness should be grabbed with both hands and hang the consequences. She threw her handbag into the broken window of the most damaged carriage in the ensuing confusion, and asked for a passage back to Sittingbourne and the arms of the ARP.

Of course to lose your identity was impossible in wartime and if she was to claim her food ration then she had to own up to being Mrs Wilton of north London. She must face up to her husband and ask for a divorce. She went to see him and heard the story of his death from a neighbour. She then spent the rest of her days wondering what on earth he was doing in a cinema south of the river.

Betty's sister Dora gave birth to a healthy baby girl, who was the pride of her grandmother. Betty and Dora tried continuously to make contact with the baby's father through clairvoyance. This always failed, convincing them both that he was still alive. Their mother made enquiries through the proper channels which eventually confirmed that the séances were uncalled for. He turned up again in

1946, married Dora and settled in Battersea. Dora often complained that he didn't take her home to Gloucestershire but his response was always the same – that he never wanted to see a muddy field again.

William Turner went the way of his cinema; he was stood in the foyer as the doodlebug landed just feet away. He wasn't particularly missed by anyone, except perhaps Mrs James from the box office, who had always rather admired him. Not being one for silly crushes, she had never let on to him just how much she had thought of him. This was rather a shame – a regular secret liaison would have been easily arranged and would have cheered up everyone concerned. Mary Turner wept a few silent tears for her husband, but soon bucked up. She and Joy lived on quite happily. Joy never did marry, but lived a very fulfilling life and became a nurse on the death of her mother.

Kay Clarke thanked fate for her attack on the bomb site, which had kept her away from the cinema that day. Once or twice before she had ignored warnings and not gone to the shelter and she might have done the same again. But she gave up being an usherette and got a job in Woolworth's. In October, her attacker was arrested under his full name of Karl Gustav Hulten, accused of carrying out the famous cleft chin murder. He was found guilty and hung. Although a little perturbed at being attacked by a murderer, she revelled in the attention it brought her and profits at her Woolworth's counter went up no end. Kay married a Greek waiter in 1950.

Bob McDonald's resolve to see more of the world was strengthened by the death of his buddy. After a spell in mainland Europe he made it home and was able to present his wife with her poetry book. He returned to his old job as a car mechanic and started up his own garage. He did well, and spent his money on travel. In 1962 he brought his wife and teenage son to London and tried to act knowledgeable as he showed them the sights. He took them across Hungerford Bridge and tried desperately to find the cinema that he had visited on the day in 1944. He couldn't even find the street where it had stood.

Miriam Hedley continued to teach in inner London until 1947, when she left to open her own school in Sussex. Her friend Anne, a war widow, joined her as assistant. They ran a well loved establishment for many years, and even though Anne married again the law finally allowed her to continue working. The school's reputation spread and Miriam was asked to take in some American pupils. Anne talked her into accepting them. She even grew to rather like them.

Printed in Great Britain
by Amazon